WEAPONS OF WAR

WEAPONS OF

WORLD

WAR II

BY MATT DOEDEN

CAPSTONE PRESS
a capstone imprint

Blazers Books are published by Capstone Press,
1710 Roe Crest Drive, North Mankato, Minnesota 56003
www.mycapstone.com

Library of Congress Cataloging-in-Publication Data
Names: Doeden, Matt, author.
Title: Weapons of World War II / by Matt Doeden
Description: North Mankato, Minnesota: Capstone Press, [2017] | Series: Blazers. Weapons of
   War | Includes bibliographical references and index.
Identifiers: ISBN 978-1-5157-7906-3 (library hardcover) | ISBN 978-1-5157-7917-9 (eBook PDF)
Subjects: LCSH: Military weapons—History—20th century—Juvenile literature.
   World War, 1939–1945—Equipment and supplies—Juvenile literature.
Classification: UF500 .D685 2018
LC record available at https://lccn.loc.gov/2016055796

Editorial Credits
Bradley Cole, editor; Kyle Grenz, designer; Jo Miller, media researcher;
Gene Bendthal, production specialist

Printed and bound in China
PO004598

TABLE OF CONTENTS

A Bloody War 4

Guns and Grenades 8
Small Arms 13

Bigger Weapons 14
Large Weapons 20

Deadly Vehicles 22
Vehicles 28

Glossary 30
Read More 31
Internet Sites 31
Index 32

A Bloody War

Soldiers storm an enemy beach during a World War II (1939–1945) battle. Explosions rock the ground. Gunfire echoes.

FACT

Germany invaded Poland on September 1, 1939. This event marked the start of World War II.

U.S. soldiers storming the beach on D-Day

5

FACT

The United States entered
the war in 1941 after Japan
bombed Pearl Harbor, a
U.S. Naval base in Hawaii.

World War II (WWII) was a huge war. The **Axis powers** fought against the **Allies**. From pistols to bombs, WWII weapons caused big damage.

Axis powers—a group of countries including Germany, Italy, and Japan that fought together in World War II

Allies—a group of countries including England, France, and the United States that fought together in World War II

 a photogragh taken by a Japanese pilot of the damage of Pearl Harbor

Guns and Grenades

The most popular weapon of WWII was the rifle. Germans carried the Mauser Karabiner 98k. U.S. soldiers fired M1 Carbine rifles, and British soldiers carried Lee-Enfield rifles.

MAUSER KARABINER 98K

LEE-ENFIELD

a U.S. soldier with an M1 Carbine rifle

Pistols worked well in close fighting. The U.S. Colt .45 was lightweight and easy to handle. British soldiers often used the Webley revolver.

WEBLEY

GERMAN HAND GRENADE

The German MP40 was a small but powerful **machine gun**. The U.S. M2 was an even more powerful machine gun.

machine gun—a gun that can fire bullets quickly without needing to be reloaded

SMALL ARMS

GERMAN MP40 »

U.S. COLT .45 »

« **GERMAN P38 PISTOL**

a U.S. soldier with a mounted Browning M2HB machine gun

Bigger Weapons

Bazookas shot small rockets. Soldiers used them to blow up enemy vehicles. A bazooka blasted through 5 inches (12.7 centimeters) of metal.

a U.S. soldier with a bazooka

Field guns chattered across battlefields. Germans fired Flak field guns. U.S. soldiers shot howitzers. The British Ordnance BL 5.5 inch was a medium artillery gun.

field gun—a large, powerful gun that is sometimes called an artillery gun

top: a German Flak field gun
bottom: British 5.5-inch guns

The Germans mounted huge guns to railway cars. These guns shot 7-ton (6.4-metric ton) shells. In 1945, the United States dropped two **atomic bombs** on Japan. The bombs were named Fat Man and Little Boy.

FACT

The atomic bombs that fell on Japan killed between 80,000 and 140,000 people.

atomic bomb—a powerful bomb that destroys large areas and leaves behind harmful elements called radiation

a German railway gun

LARGE WEAPONS

⌃ FAT MAN
ATOMIC BOMB

⌃ LITTLE BOY
ATOMIC BOMB

⌃ GERMAN COASTAL GUN

GERMAN HEAVY HOWITZER

240 MM HOWITZER

GERMAN FLAK
88 MM FIELD GUN

Deadly Vehicles

Deadly vehicles roamed WWII battlefields. Tanks had huge guns and strong **armor**.

armor—a heavy metal layer on a military vehicle that protects against bullets or bombs

U.S. troops entering a Belgian town

a British Spitfire Mk V ❯❯❯❯

Warplanes filled the sky.
Japanese Zeroes battled U.S. P-51
Mustangs. German Messerschmitts
fought British Spitfires. Bombers
attacked from high above the action.

Battleships, aircraft carriers, and destroyers fought on the sea. Submarines cruised underwater. They shot enemy ships on the ocean's surface.

◄◄◄ the USS *Lexington*, a U.S. aircraft carrier

For six years, WWII raged on the Pacific Ocean and in Europe. The war's powerful weapons left a lasting mark on the world.

a destroyed U.S. tanker

torpedo—an explosive weapon that travels underwater

a U.S. Navy PT boat

Vehicles

U.S. P-40

U.S. M3 ARMORED CAR SCOUT

U.S. B-17 BOMBER

U.S. P-51 MUSTANG

BRITISH SPITFIRE

U.S. WATER BUFFALO SEA SHIP

USS *ALABAMA* BATTLESHIP

U.S. M5 LIGHT TANK

GERMAN U-BOAT

USS *CASSIN YOUNG* DESTROYER

GERMAN PANZER

Glossary

Allies (AL-lyz)—a group of countries including England, France, and the United States that fought together in World War II

armor (AR-muhr)—a heavy metal layer on a military vehicle that protects against bullets or bombs

atomic bomb (uh-TAH-mik BOM)—a powerful bomb that destroys large areas and leaves behind harmful elements called radiation

Axis powers (AK-siss POW-uhrs)—a group of countries including Germany, Italy, and Japan that fought together in World War II

field gun (FEELD GUHN)—a large, powerful gun that is sometimes called an artillery gun

machine gun (muh-SHEEN GUHN)—a gun that can fire bullets quickly without needing to be reloaded

torpedo (tor-PEE-doh)—an explosive weapon that travels underwater

Read More

Hudak, Heather C. *Technology during World War II*. Military Technologies. Minneapolis: Abdo, 2017.

Ringstad, Arnold. *World War II Weapons*. Essential Library of World War II. Minnespolis: Abdo, 2016.

Roesler, Jill. *Eyewitness to Dropping the Atomic Bombs*. Eyewitness to World War II. Mankato, Minn.: Childs World, 2016.

Internet Sites

FactHound offers a safe, fun way to find Internet sites related to this book. All of the sites on FactHound have been researched by our staff.

Here's all you do:

Visit *www.facthound.com*

Type in this code: 978515779063

Super-cool stuff!

Check out projects, games and lots more at
www.capstonekids.com

Index

Allies, 7

armor, 22

artillery guns

  see field guns

Axis powers, 7

bazookas, 14

bombs, 7, 18

field guns, 17

  Flak guns, 17

  howitzers, 17

Germany, 4

grenades, 10–11

Japan, 6, 18

machine guns, 12

  M2, 12

  MP40, 12

Pearl Harbor, 6

pistols, 7–11

  Colt .45, 11

  Webley, 11

rifles, 8

  Lee-Enfield, 8

  M1 Carbine, 8

  Mauser Karabiner 98k, 8

ships, 25

  aircraft carriers, 25, 27

  battleships, 25

  destroyers, 25

  Patrol Torpedo (PT) boats, 27

  submarines, 25

tanks, 22

torpedoes, 27

United States, 6, 18

vehicles, 14, 22

  airplanes, 24

    Messerschmitt 24

    P-51 Mustang 24

    Spitfire 24

    Zero 24